# I CAN
# SEE
## Peter Curry

Published by Price/Stern/Sloan Publishers, Inc.
410 North La Cienega Boulevard, Los Angeles, California 90048
Text and illustrations copyright© 1982 by Peter Curry

ISBN: 0-8431-0947-5
Printed in Hong Kong

### PRICE/STERN/SLOAN
*Publishers, Inc., Los Angeles*
**1984**

# I have two eyes to see with.

I can look where I am going
and not bump into the table or chairs.

I can see my fingers
close up in front of my eyes,

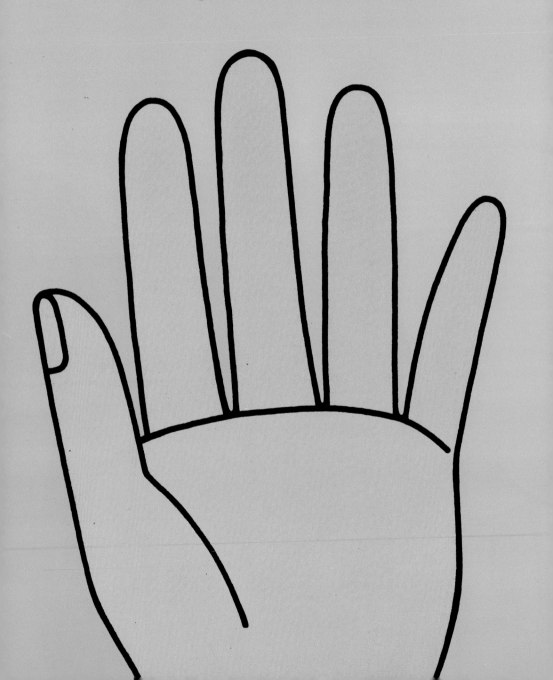

**and I can see the clouds
way up in the sky.**

**I can see colors:
bright red and yellow, green and blue,**

**dark black, light white,
pale gray and dull brown.**

**I can see shapes:
a triangle, a circle,
oblongs and a square.**

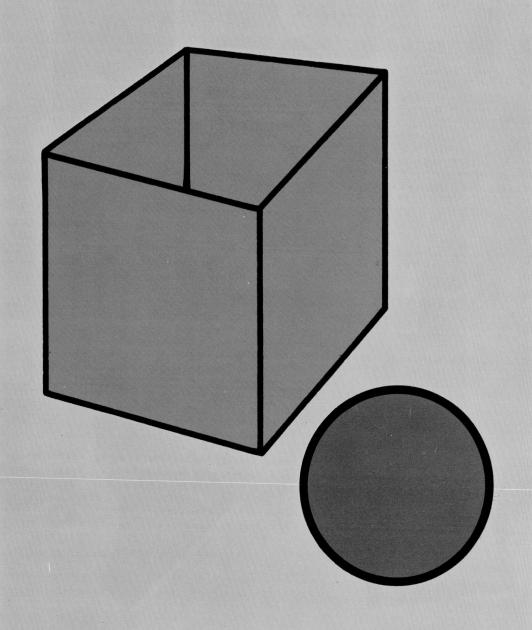

**I can see the shape
of a box and my ball.**

**I can look to see
where the jigsaw pieces go,**

**and I can look for
my ball when it's lost.**

**I can look at my car
to see its shape from all sides,**

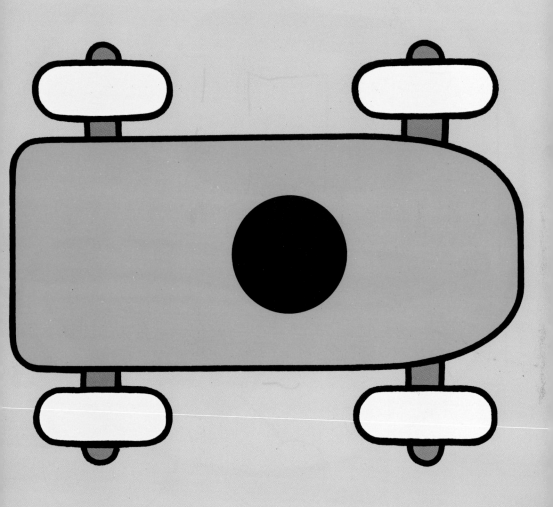

**the front and the back,
the top and the bottom.**

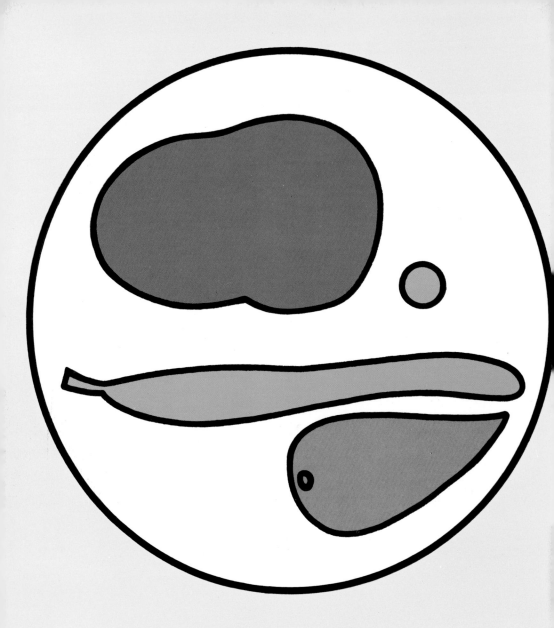

**I can see a big potato
beside a little pea,
and a long, thin bean
next to a short, fat carrot.**

I can see trees growing high
and the grass growing low,
a wide road, and a narrow path.

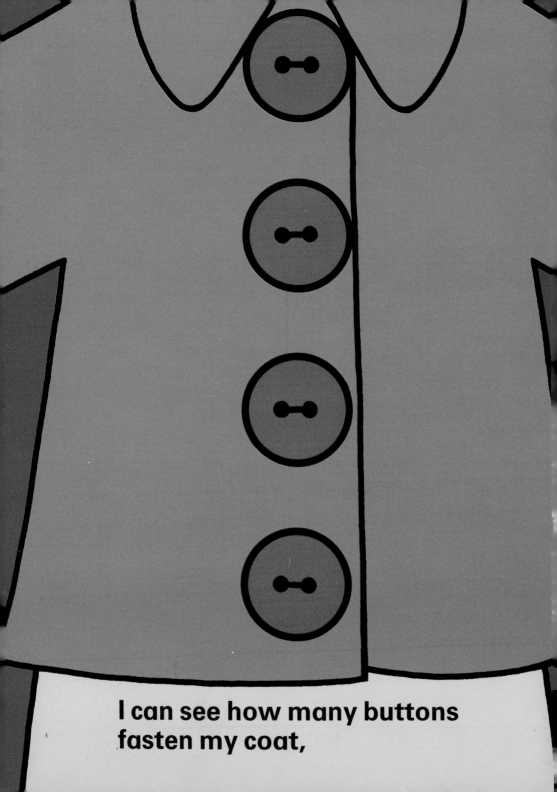

I can see how many buttons
fasten my coat,

**and if two socks make a pair**

**I can see when a cup
stands upside-down,**

**and if my bricks
are in a long straight row.**

The little pony ran as fast as he could.

I can look at a book to see pictures and words on the pages,

**and watch television, where pictures move on the screen.**

**I can watch a top
spinning round and round,**

**and my clown
rocking from side to side.**

I can see myself
when I look in a mirror,

**and my shadow on the ground
if I stand in the sun.**

I can see the different colored lights which tell the traffic when to stop, wait or go,

and the sign which shows the way.

I can see outside through the window,
and just by looking
I know if it's wet and windy
or sunny and dry.

I can watch people seem to grow smaller
as they walk further away.
By looking carefully,
I can tell if someone has been shopping.

I can play remembering games.
I look very hard at things on a tray
and, when some of them
are taken secretly away,
I try to remember what they are.

I can make pictures of the things I see,
with lines and colors,
shapes and patterns.

# I can't see in the dark!
# Please switch on the light.